Praise for Mary Conley and
FIRST COUSINS AT THE FARM . . .

"Mary Conley has been a Capper's Farmer blogger since 2013, and her writings are always informational and entertaining. In her children's book *First Cousins at the Farm*, she shares the adventures and learning experiences on the farm through the eyes of today's youth, and also incorporates memories of the good old days throughout the pages."

-Capper's Farmer editors

"In the spirit of *In Grandma's Attic* and the *Little House on the Prairie* series, Mary Conley writes a delightful book *First Cousins at the Farm*, an engaging story about children going back to their grandparents' farm and a simple lifestyle. Entertaining, highly delightful and memory-evoking, this book is sure to please every age of reader."

-Kathy Cortinas, homeschool mom

"Mary Conley has written a lovely book that is certain to bring joy to her friends and family for years to come."

-Summer Miller, Author of New Prairie Kitchen

FIRST COUSINS
AT THE
FARM

A FIRST COUSIN SHENANIGAN BOOK

MARY CONLEY

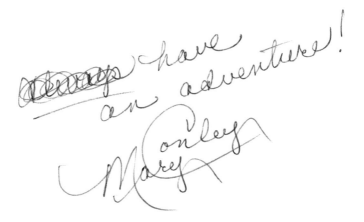

always have an adventure!
Mary Conley

ELECTRIC
MOON
PUBLISHING

www.emoonpublishing.com

First Cousins at the Farm: A First Cousin Shenanigan Book © 2017
Mary Conley

Published by Electric Moon Publishing, LLC
An author-friendly, custom publishing place
Stromsburg, NE
www.emoonpublishing.com
info@emoonpublishing.com

Paperback
ISBN-10: 1-943027-21-8
ISBN-13: 978-1-943027-21-7

E-book
ISBN-10: 1-943027-22-6
ISBN-13: 978-1-943027-22-4

Cover Design: Lyn Rayn, Electric Moon Publishing Creative Art
Department

Printed in the United States of America

www.emoonpublishing.com

DEDICATION

I dedicate this book to my delightful
grandchildren, who allowed me to mix their
characters with fact and fiction.

Hi, kids! You may wonder if this book is fact or fiction. Well, it is both. The descriptions of the cousins are true with a few exceptions that only family and close friends will notice. The grandparents' stories are completely true, as are the references to the great grandparents. (You may want to ask your grandparents to tell you their stories sometime.) The places on the farm are real, and much of the book is built upon happenings experienced there.

CONTENTS

ACKNOWLEDGMENTS

I want to thank . . .

My friend Kathy Cortinas for reading my book early on and calling it worthy to be published.

My son Perry, who gave me some initial suggestions.

My daughter Amy, who read it through twice for light editing.

My granddaughter Katie, who has grown up since her part in the book, and did additional editing with fear and trembling that she might hurt her grandma's feelings.

Then there are the many family and friends who greatly encouraged me.

Most of all, I want to thank my husband Larry, who read each new story out loud with feeling and enthusiasm—many times. He was always supportive and constructive. Well, except for the time I wrote how our granddaughter cried in the story. "You can't make my Katie cry!" he said.

I rewrote that part.

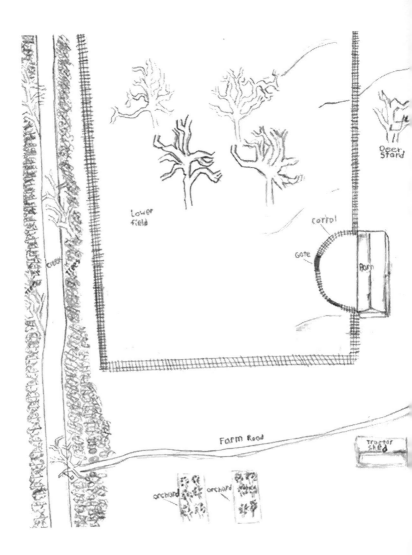

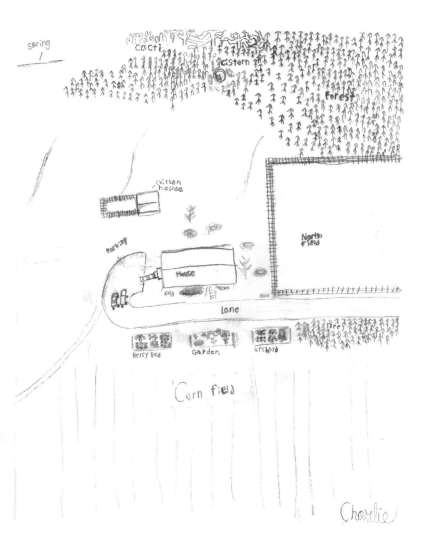

MEET THE COUSINS

I've heard it said your *first* best friends are probably your cousins. That is, if you are fortunate enough to have some. The lucky characters in my story are a group of nine first cousins. Yes, there are nine of them and they are all about the same age. To be first cousins, some of their parents have to be brothers or sisters. It also means they have several aunts and uncles watching over them. Most importantly, they are my grandchildren.

You can imagine what an interesting group these cousins are with their different personalities. They always experience excitement when they are together, and they are the best of friends. Having been taught to be polite and kind, they rarely make a fuss. Instead, they use their collective knowledge and insights to create exciting fun. I would like to tell you a little about each of them before I begin our story.

FAMILY #1: JOSHUA AND THE TWINS: KATIE AND CALEB
(ALSO KNOWN AS DOUBLE TROUBLE)

Joshua

Joshua is thirteen and he is the oldest. You need to imagine him as tall with brown hair and brown eyes because that is the way he looks! He has always had a great imagination. When he was little, he created an imaginary friend named Crodia. She had dark skin and was from Spain. Because she was invisible, Joshua watched over her carefully so no one would sit on her. Crodia was given the top bunk to sleep in at night and was buckled safely in the car on trips. When the twins were born, Crodia went back to Spain, but Joshua kept his imagination.

He has a mechanical mind and is very active in robotics. I expect he'll do great things someday. He is the typical oldest child in his family, which means he is responsible. That handsome boy is my favorite.

Katie

Oh, you should have seen Katie when she was little. She was cute as a bug and had big brown eyes and wispy brown hair. She walked early—ran, really—and had a naughty streak.

"Quite defiant," were her mommy's exact words.

I once saw her put her hands on her hips, stomp her foot, and shout "No!" when told to be nice.

Katie was also adventurous and got into one thing after another. Her mommy had to call poison control twice: once when she drank perfume and once when she ate a leaf off my houseplant. I thought it would be a wonder if she lived long enough to become an adult. Katie is already ten but she's no longer naughty. She is still adventurous, though, and quite a delight. She is definitely my favorite.

Caleb

Yes, you guessed it. Caleb also has brown hair and brown eyes. So, what is unique about him? Well, of all my grandchildren, he was the naughtiest when he was little, and even the most handsome little boy is not likable if he doesn't behave himself. He even got in trouble more often than his twin.

Let me give you an example: One time, when the whole extended family was together at our house, Caleb walked over to his Uncle Todd, picked up a big bowl of popcorn, and dumped it on the floor. On purpose. You should have seen Todd's face. His expression made it clear that he didn't like Caleb very much right then. His mommy and daddy were embarrassed and decided to put in a lot of effort to make sure Caleb was not allowed to get away with any more mischief. The good news is that it worked.

He is always sorry if he misbehaves, which is seldom, and he is very loving. He likes woodworking and anything mechanical. Caleb has grown into a helpful, energetic, and well-behaved ten-year-old boy. In fact, he is my favorite.

FAMILY #2: ALLISON, ERIN, AND MOLLY

Allison

Allison is twelve and the oldest girl of the cousins. For this family, you must change your imagination to blue eyes and light brown hair. And curls. Allison has gorgeous long curls. She is our wordy grandchild. I know it is difficult to believe, but she taught herself to read when she was only three. She already knew the alphabet and a few letter sounds, but unbeknownst to her parents, she memorized the words as they read to her.

One night at bedtime, her daddy read half of *Charlotte's Web*. The next night, as he was about to read the last half, she informed him they needed to choose another book because she had finished that one at nap time. He questioned her and sure enough, she knew how to read. It makes me wonder if she will become a famous writer when she grows up. You can understand why she is my favorite.

Erin

Erin is eleven and yes, she has blue eyes and light brown hair, too. Only her curls are short. When she and Allison were small, they shared a love for horses. They read about them, played with their horse play set, and made saddle blankets. I often saw them galloping around on their hands and knees pretending they were horses. Then one day, the girls received a surprise. No, they didn't get a horse, but they did get to take riding lessons.

A real horse is quite different from reading about one, but Erin discovered she is a true lover of horses. She can ride and ride, even alone, and never get bored. Erin has also been good with her hands from the time she was little and could dress Bitty Baby Doll all by herself. She could even handle the buttons. So, it doesn't surprise me how good she can crochet, already. She reminds me of my mother, her great-grandmother Edith, who loved to crochet. So naturally, she is my favorite.

Molly

Molly is nine, and she also has . . . well, actually she doesn't have blue eyes and light brown, curly hair. She has brown hair and big brown eyes. You would almost think she could fit in the same family as Josh, Katie, and Caleb. Well, that is because she is adopted. Her parents didn't just walk into an orphanage and choose the cutest baby, though. No, it isn't that easy. They went to an adoption agency. It takes a lot of time and money to adopt a baby, so, if you are adopted like Molly, you know your parents really, really want you.

Molly was born with hip dysplasia, and although she has had several operations, she walks with a limp. She is a contented, happy girl, though, and makes everyone laugh. Her hobbies are drawing and shaping things out of clay. Oh, I almost forgot: Molly has a real talent for playing the piano. I used to be a piano teacher, so it's no wonder she is my favorite.

FAMILY #3: CHARLIE, SOPHIE, AND ELLIOTT

We've come to the third family of kids. I'm just going to tell you up front that they all three have very, very blond hair and blue eyes. They are also homeschooled.

Charlie

Charlie is nine and has braces. His teeth are starting to look great, but I can barely understand him because he talks so fast. He is artistic and loves dragons, Legos, and *Star Wars* movies. And you should see his Pokémon card collection. Actually, he collects and keeps many things.

Reading is near the top of Charlie's list of favorite things to do, and he is about finished with the *Harry Potter* books.

He has a great sense of humor and keeps us entertained with jokes.

An outdoor-adventure class instructor showed him how to make the best paper airplanes, even out-flying those that Grandpa makes. Charlie is a nature kid and is outside as often as possible, which, of course, makes him my favorite.

Sophie

Sophie was a typical little girl, playing with her dolls and doll house. Now, at age eight, she and her friend play with American Girl Dolls.

Sophie loves to dance, and Grandpa and I go to her dance recitals.

Just like Charlie, she is quite artistic, likes to play outside, and ride bikes.

When Sophie was a baby, she didn't let Grandpa or me hold her. She only liked her mommy. It was very disappointing.

Much to our surprise, she turned into a very loving little girl. In fact, I think Sophie gives us more hugs and kisses than all the other grandchildren put together. You can see why she is my favorite.

Elliott

Elliott is the youngest of the cousins, and only six years old. He could hold his own from the time he was two-and-a-half if older kids tried to take advantage of him. He never got mad but he was quick to tell them how it was. Yes, Elliott could do that because he already had a good vocabulary and knew how to use it. His early usage of words both astounded us and made us laugh at times.

He also seemed to be naturally aware of danger and what he could or could not do safely. That was a good thing because he was also very active.

Elliott is still very grown up for his age but not always enough to keep up with his older cousins. When you imagine him, remember that he is not only the "little kid" in the bunch but he has the cutest face with blue twinkly eyes and a round head, covered with short, curly hair. I have a photo of my father, Elliott's great-grandfather, Charley— when he was little. He also had a round head with short, curly hair, and twinkly eyes. You guessed it, Elliott is my favorite.

Now that you've been introduced to each of the nine first cousins, have you already thought about how much fun they are going to have in our story? What helps make this possible is the important thing I mentioned at the very beginning. Remember? They have been taught how to be polite and kind. But what if they do have a fight? Will it spoil everything? Well, there was the time when . . .

The whole family was at our house on Christmas Eve a few years ago. Of course, everyone is nice on Christmas Eve. Well, it had been a long, exciting day, and it was way past young Charlie's bedtime. He felt tired and crabby and wasn't talking nicely to cousin Molly. In fact, he was being downright bossy.

Uh oh! His mommy and daddy heard him and took him upstairs for a little chat. When he came back down, he went straight over to Molly and told her he was sorry. Molly immediately put her arms around him in a big, first-cousin hug and said, "I forgive you."

Yes, at a very young age our grandchildren have not only learned how to apologize but also how to forgive. Those are important things to know, and they might come in handy in our story about the nine first cousins at our farm. Let's begin.

PART ONE

PREFACE

VISITING THE FARM

All of the nine first cousins lived in or near the city of Omaha, Nebraska, where Grandpa and I used to live. So, it completely surprised them when we bought a small hobby farm. After all, we were getting old.

"Why do you want to work more when you could be retiring?" our grown children asked. Grandpa and I were in complete agreement on buying the farm, though, and were as happy as we could be. We planted all kinds of fruit and nut trees, berries, gardens, and everything we could think of that would grow in our climate. We also had a few animals.

"Animals make a farm come alive," I often said.

So, we had chickens for organic eggs, a few meat chickens, and a cow for fresh milk.

"Sure, Grandma wanted a cow, and guess who milks that cow morning and night?" Grandpa said with a twinkle in his eyes.

I always smiled every time he said that, knowing he liked to do it—almost as much as he liked to complain about it.

I wanted bees, too. Bees always fascinated me.

Grandpa hoped to add a couple of pigs and maybe some pygmy goats.

We wanted to experience *everything*. The cousins, of course, wanted horses to ride when they visited, but we told them horses were far too expensive.

You can imagine it was an exciting time for the nine first cousins when we invited them all to come to the farm for the last two weeks before school started.

Mercy, I must have needed my head examined. What was I thinking? Grandpa had to continually reassure me that the grandkids, ages six to thirteen, were old enough to take care of themselves and to help with the cooking and cleanup after each meal.

Still, it would take a truckload of food to feed everyone for two whole weeks. And what about all the dirty laundry from playing and working outside? Again, Grandpa reminded me they had all agreed to work a little each day as part of the deal.

And, of course, he would help, too.

ARRIVING
AT THE FARM

The cousins began arriving on a hot Saturday morning, and their parents stayed until after lunch. I overheard Allison, Erin, and Molly being given a suggestion.

"Grandma and Grandpa won't be around forever, so this will be a perfect opportunity to listen carefully to their special stories," their daddy said.

Molly thought it would be a good bedtime ritual and soon told the others. They elected Allison to record the stories each night since she was the writer of the family.

"I'm going to jot down some of their weird sayings," Erin said. She had a mischievous grin that gave away her ornery side.

Before the parents left to return home, Caleb and Katie were given instructions from their dad. "Twins," he warned in a stern voice. "*No* shenanigans."

Grandpa had his own philosophy about how to raise children. He thought they should be outside working, play-ing, and learning something. "The best self-esteem comes from knowing how to do many things and to be able to take care of yourself in all situations," he often said.

I agreed, and besides outdoor activities, I wanted to start the girls on learning how to crochet and embroider.

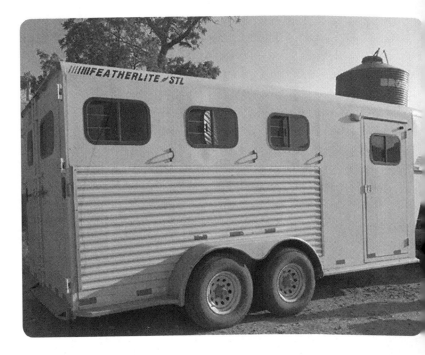

About mid-afternoon, we heard a commotion coming down the lane. The cousins all rushed out to find a truck pulling a horse trailer. Tracey, a neighbor, was bringing three of her horses and everything we needed to feed and ride them. In exchange, Grandpa had agreed to let the horses graze his pastures until late fall.

"Horses!" Katie exclaimed. "Yay, horses! Do we get to ride them?"

Tracey backed the horses out of the trailer as the cousins all watched.

"Whoa, they are really big," Elliott said, and he backed away, too.

"And smelly," Sophie said as one of the horses did his business right in front of them. "That is rude. Why do such beautiful animals have to poop?"

"You poop," Josh said. Then he laughed and watched her face turn red.

"I'll show you where I keep a shovel and wheelbarrow for such occasions," Grandpa said. "I expect you to keep the yard and lane cleaned up if you ride the horses out here."

Allison, Erin, and Molly each quickly grabbed the reins of a horse and started for the corral. They had taken riding lessons and knew what to do. Tracey and the others began lugging the equipment and heavy saddles to the tack room of the barn.

"I can't believe we get to learn how to ride horses," Charlie said. "Mom and Dad will be so surprised when I call them."

Tracey stayed and taught the cousins about horse safety and demonstrated how to saddle and mount up. Since there were nine cousins, they could take turns each day going out three at a time to ride in the countryside.

"These horses need riding, so I'm glad you are here," Tracey said. "I'll stop in again in the morning for another lesson."

As she got back into the truck, I gave her some jars of homemade jellies and jams and thanked her for her patience with the grandkids.

"Boys, we have an important job to do," Grandpa said.

So, Josh, Caleb, Charlie, and Elliott walked with him down along the lower pasture fence, following it all the way along Sappa Creek and up the hill to make sure the horses couldn't get out.

"Could the horses jump over the fence?" Caleb asked.

"They aren't used to jumping, so I don't think they'll try," Grandpa replied.

Next, they trimmed a few low branches off the trees for the safety of both the horses and riders. When they finished, they let the horses out of the corral to graze in the pasture.

"Look at them go!" Charlie shouted.

Then the horses started rolling in the grass, making us all laugh!

In the late evening, we all went out to the corral. Grandpa filled a small feed pan with kernels of corn and gave it to

Josh. "Shake this hard," he said. Soon the horses heard the noise and came running. Their hooves sounded like thunder as they came up over the bank.

"I'm getting out of here!" Katie yelled.

Everyone quickly climbed over the corral fence until the horses settled down. After they ate and drank, Grandpa coaxed them into the barn and closed the door. They would get used to their new place and be safe for the night.

Back in the house, the cousins soon discovered it was quite an ordeal taking turns showering. "Girls take far too long," Caleb complained. "We boys should always go first."

Grandpa saved the day—rather, the night—by setting out puzzles and games on card tables. Soon, everyone quieted and realized how tired they were from their first big day at the farm. When I said it was time for bed because tomorrow would be just as big, Allison had a request.

"Grandpa and Grandma," she said, "we wish for you to tell us a story each night. Tell us something we don't know about your lives."

Grandpa decided he would go first, so when everyone was in their pajamas and had their teeth brushed, he told about how a boy's childhood was different back in his day.

GRANDPA'S CHILDHOOD

Grandpa

"Well, I had the most perfect childhood any boy could wish for," Grandpa said. "I was allowed to leave the house and play anywhere all day."

"Unsupervised?" Josh asked.

"Oh, yes," Grandpa replied. "I could stay in our small town of Washta, Iowa, where I knew who lived in nearly every house, go fishing and swimming in the town's pond and the Little Sioux River, or roam the woods playing Cowboys and Indians. I could go anywhere with my friends as long as I stayed out of trouble and was back home by mealtime."

"Grandpa, I can't believe you could have such freedom," Erin said. "Weren't your parents afraid something terrible might happen to you? You could have drowned in the river, or fallen out of a tree."

"Well, nothing bad ever happened to me, and I don't remember any of my friends getting hurt, either," Grandpa answered. "We had a great time."

"We could never do that," Caleb muttered. "Our parents would worry the whole time we were gone."

The grandkids were quiet. It was a lot to think about.

We had never purchased extra beds, which worked out nicely. The boys shared two large air mattresses in the smaller bedroom, and the girls shared two, plus an extra single one in the big bedroom.

"I'll take the single mattress by the door," Allison said. "I don't want to bother you with my diabetes routine."

Yes, I'm sorry to say that our sweet Allison became a diabetic when she was a toddler. So, before going to sleep each night, she needed to poke her finger with a needle to test her blood sugar and then call her mom and dad to make sure she gave herself the right amount of insulin. She went to diabetes camp earlier in the summer and along with many other diabetic children, learned to give herself insulin injections.

Coming to the farm for two weeks was quite a responsibility for her. I helped keep Allison well by setting my alarm each night and going into her room with a flashlight to poke her finger and check her blood sugar. I decided that if her daddy had done this since she was fourteen months old, surely, I could do it for two weeks.

The difficult part was the luggage. The boys managed to keep theirs heaped on the closet floor. After all, what did they need on a farm besides underclothes, a couple pairs of jeans, and a few worn-out t-shirts? The girls, however, had their bags lined up all down the hallway.

"Women!" Grandpa said.

"Women!" the boys echoed.

As you would expect, there was all kinds of nonsense going on for a while, but eventually the cousins quieted enough to fall asleep, listening to the far-off eerie yipping of the coyotes.

"What's that?" Elliott whispered.

"A big pack of wolves coming to eat you," his brother answered. "Go to sleep."

SPECIAL PROJECTS

Grandpa had a plan to rotate everyone, two by two, doing the chores each morning and night, so everyone could learn and experience the farm. Animals had to be fed and let out in the morning, then fed and put back in at night. Eggs needed to be gathered, and water containers had to be kept filled. The garden would need to be weeded now and then, and the produce picked and cleaned. He explained all this over breakfast.

"That sounds like a lot of work," Charlie moaned.

"With all of us doing our part, there will still be plenty of play time," Grandpa said.

Then everyone set out to get the chores finished before Tracey came for their second riding lesson.

"Hi, everyone," Tracey greeted. "Let's see what you remember from yesterday."

The cousins were quick to learn and apply her instructions, and it was decided that either Allison or Erin would supervise getting the horses saddled each day to prevent an accident. Only Allison, Josh, and Erin managed to mount from the ground, so Tracey taught the others how to walk the horse over to the fence so they could climb it to get on. Elliott's leg still couldn't reach the horse, which had everyone giggling.

"Jump!" the cousins shouted.

"No way," he said as he hung tightly onto the fence.

Grandpa promised to help him on and off each time it was his turn to ride.

"Only ride in the lower pasture until you feel comfortable going out in the countryside," he said.

Because riding was new and hard on the legs, most of them only lasted about a half an hour, which gave everyone a turn before it was lunch time.

Sophie hugged and kissed us multiple times for the experience. "Thank you, thank you, thank you. I love the horses. They are so beautiful and gentle."

"And big," Elliott added.

After lunch, Grandpa took the boys out to start their special project. The barn loft needed a new floor, and with much grunting and groaning, Josh and Caleb helped him carry up a few big sheets of OSB—similar to plywood—to lay on top of the existing floor. Then they all began learning two skills Grandpa thought were important to know: how to use a hammer and a drill.

"I love this power drill," Josh said as he drove in a screw and then took it out.

Soon, Caleb and Charlie mastered the techniques, too.

"Cool," Elliott said, although his screw went in crooked.

Using the hammer, however, was a whole different story. It was heavy and their arms quickly tired.

"Ouch," and similar words were yelled when they missed the nail and hit a thumb or finger. It really hurt.

"Practice makes perfect," Grandpa said. "You will become experts with the hammer if you repeat this process over and over each day until the floor is finished."

Charlie wasn't nearly as certain. "It's too hard for me," he mumbled. Then he noticed his little brother, Elliott, was quite determined.

In the meantime, I started teaching the girls to crochet. I had already shown Allison and Erin how to do the basic stitches, so I surprised them with enough yarn and instructions to make a lovely neck scarf for next winter. It was also a gift for them because I knew they would be helpful in teaching the other girls.

"Oh, Grandma!" Allison exclaimed. "I love the color. I can hardly wait to get started."

"Mine is pretty, too," Erin said, "but it's a new pattern. Do you really think I can do it, Grandma?"

It didn't take Katie, Molly, and Sophie long to become tired and frustrated, so we quit after a short time. I encouraged them to not give up but to remember that it would become easier and easier each day. I also had plans to teach them how to embroider, so today I gave them each their own pillow case with a picture stamped on it.

"Wow! We are going to be regular *Little House on the Prairie* girls by the time we leave," Allison said as they picked out colors of embroidery thread and learned to thread a needle and tie a knot.

"Grandma and I are going to take a nap, and you might want to stay inside from this horrible heat," Grandpa said after lunch.

After they rested, Grandpa suggested they do chores and help with supper earlier than usual so everyone could head down to the creek for a couple of hours before nightfall. He had rigged up a swing over the deepest part, and they couldn't wait to try it out.

"The oldest gets to go first!" Joshua shouted, and off he swung back and forth.

"I'm the oldest girl," Allison said, and grabbed the swing next.

"Look at me!" Charlie hung upside down and did other antics.

"Showoff!" his sister yelled. "Oh, that is *so* Charlie."

Everyone took turns, even though it was scary at first for some of them. Oh, but they had so much fun! One of the boys stayed on each side of the creek to help anyone

who needed it. Sure enough, Molly was afraid to turn loose, and as she swung back and forth, the swing slowed until it didn't quite make it to the side of the creek. She nervously looked way down at the deep water and became very frightened.

"What should I do?" she cried out.

Josh quickly came to the rescue and stuck a long branch out for her to grab with one hand, and then he pulled her and the swing over to the bank so Caleb could help her off.

Molly was quite upset from it all and a few tears ran down her cheeks. Soon, she calmed down, but she was embarrassed.

"How about trying it once more, Molly, so you won't feel defeated?" Josh said. "We'll help you."

She bravely set off again, and when the swing returned, they all hollered "Now!" She let her feet touch the ground. Caleb grabbed a hold of the swing until she got off.

"Yay, Molly!" they all cheered. The cousins knew outdoor activities weren't always easy for Molly as her hips and legs didn't work perfectly.

"I'm glad I didn't give up," she said, "and I'll try it again next time we come, if you help me."

Along with taking turns on the creek swing, there was a lot to see and do in the area. Grandpa pointed out the nettles that can make one really itch, and the rusty barbed

wire coming out of the ground here and there where an old fence had fallen down years ago. He also showed them a high bank where the current had washed the dirt out underneath.

"You need to be aware of such places and learn not to stand on the edge of a bank where it might crumble underneath you," he said. "It is good to know how to take care of yourself so you can have a great time discovering nature."

When the mosquitoes came out, we all knew it was time to get back to the house and ready for bed.

WHEN GRANDPA WAS A BOY

Grandpa

It was story time again, but immediately, the children had questions.

"Did you have toys, Grandpa?" Elliott asked.

"Oh, yes," Grandpa answered, "but mostly learning toys, such as building blocks, Tinker Toys, Lincoln Logs, and an Erector Set."

"What games did you play?" Caleb asked.

"Well, I can remember a couple of board games, but my favorite was playing marbles," Grandpa recalled. "We boys played marbles before school, at recess, and every chance we got. I would rather show you that game instead of telling you about it."

"How come we don't have freedom like you did?" Josh asked. "Even my dad got to roam the mountains of Colorado with his siblings, and I know you let your kids have freedom because Mom is always telling us stories about how she and her brothers got to play in a creek, dig forts, and build tree houses in vacant lots.

"And explore the storm sewers around their neighborhood with a flashlight," Caleb added. "Mom told us about it."

Grandpa smiled at those memories which seemed like yesterday, but he needed to try and give them an answer to that difficult question.

"First of all," he said, "I lived in a small farming town where everyone knew each other, while you live in or near a big city. Also, because the population has increased, so has the number of bad people. But, I think many parents have become overly protective and there should still be a lot of outdoor fun that goes beyond supervised sports. Kids need to be outside playing in the neighborhood after school instead of in the house watching TV and gaming. I also believe that parents should make exploring nature a priority; they should go for walks in parks and to the many lakes and rivers."

"We all do those things," Katie said.

"Grandpa," Allison said, "I remember how we all played with your big oatmeal container full of marbles when we were small."

"I still do," Elliott interrupted.

"Now we know where they all came from," Allison continued.

"Yes, I bought many of them, but I won my fair share," Grandpa said with a smile as he remembered. "How about tomorrow we make a game circle and a marble pot under the shade of a big tree and I'll show you how to play?"

They couldn't wait to get started.

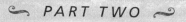

PART TWO

FREEDOM

A DECISION

Grandma

I'm sure you know I'm the one who has been telling this story. Well, it is about to change. You see, after the cousins went to bed that second night, Grandpa and I talked about the grandkids' need to be independent, to have more freedom. They continually came back to that subject, and Grandpa and I know how important it is for adults to give children the chance to experience growing-up opportunities. We need to respect their ability to be wise in their decisions, even if they occasionally make the wrong ones.

So, the next morning, there was a change of plans. What a surprise for them to hear they could do whatever they wanted, and when they wanted, with exception of taking care of the chores and animals. We gave them three rules: they should never go off alone, always wear their shoes, even when wading in mud or water, and be back by mealtime.

Grandpa and I thought it would be interesting and gratifying for us to watch them work out their own plans for the chores and free time. Consequently, my writing this account has come nearly to an end, because, you see, I wasn't always there when they made plans and had their adventures. I guess we'll have to let them help tell the story.

Joshua

That morning at breakfast, our grandparents gave us what they called "the gift of freedom," and as I left the house, I was sure my dad was in my head telling me once more that with freedom comes responsibility. It must be the thing about being the oldest child in our family because right away, I began to worry. I was afraid that with so many of us, something might get left undone. I cringed thinking we might forget to leave water for any of the animals on these hot summer days, so I suggested we have a little meeting after chores each morning and evening to make certain we hadn't neglected anything. I don't want to be responsible for *everything,* though, or seem bossy.

Allison

Erin and I continued being in charge of saddling the horses today, although we won't need to much longer since everyone caught on quickly. She and I agreed to take turns checking the horses over each evening for any cuts or injuries.

Erin

I started my list of Grandma's and Grandpa's sayings, and plan to print a copy for everyone before we leave. So far, for Grandma I have: *fiddlesticks, what on earth, mercy, lollygagging,* and *goodness, gracious, sakes alive.* With only two bathrooms for all of us, she often says, "Now don't be dilly-dallying in there." Most often, she says, "For Pete sakes." Then Grandpa corrects her and says, "Mary, it's for Pete's sake." But she never changes and he never stops correcting her. We all just look at each other thinking, "Here they go again."

Grandpa likes to say *hogwash* and *humdinger.* When he goes out to work he says, "Time to get cracking."

What surprises me is, when we leave the house, Grandma never tells us to be careful like most moms and grandmas. She always says something like: "Have an adventure," "Learn something new," "Find some magic," or "Don't forget to smell." When she says, "Be inquisitive," or "Be aware of your surroundings," I always leave feeling curious, like a question mark is in a bubble above my head, and I wonder what the day will bring.

Molly

I'm glad I learned to be content doing quieter things those many times I was in a cast when I was small because sometimes it is difficult to keep up with the others even though they are helpful and patient with me. Surprisingly, after my first scary encounter, I found I love to swing over the creek. Sophie and Elliott do, too, and we usually take off right after chores, unless it is our turn to go riding. I don't need anyone to help me get off when I reach the bank anymore, and if the swing slows down, I pump and pump to get myself to the edge again. After a couple turns, though, I become tired and we investigate the area. It is interesting what you can find under a log. Especially for Elliott, who loves bugs.

Elliott

Boy, Mom and Dad are going to be surprised at my bug collection. First thing Mom will say is, "Where are you going to put them all?" I know she'll be interested, though, because she is the one who gave me a book about bugs for my birthday and reminded me to bring it with me. Caleb likes bugs, too, and when he found a hard, empty cicada shell, he attached it to the bill of my cap. I had more fun startling the girls.

Grandma

This day certainly went fast, and the first thing we knew, it was story time again. Our previous stories about Grandpa's childhood got us reminiscing about when we were young, and we thought the grandkids might find other things about those days of interest.

REMINISCING

Grandma

Grandpa remembers how he rode his bike all over the town and countryside and left it here and there while off adventuring. The kids back then didn't even know what a bike lock was, and no one took someone else's bike unless it was a joke or prank.

In our small-town school, we never worried about anyone stealing. We kept everything in our desks in grade school, and in our study hall desks in the older grades. We had combination locks on our lockers for high school sports, but we never used them. I'm not good at remembering numbers, so I didn't even try to remember my combination. One time, my lock got closed accidentally and I had to ask the coach to look up my combination. He wasn't happy with me when it happened a second time.

In our farmhouse, the outside doors had key locks that we never used, not even at night or when we were gone for the day. I once asked my mom— your great-grandmother, Edith—where they kept the keys. She couldn't remember. "Oh, they're around here somewhere," she said.

Concerning our vehicles, we not only didn't lock the doors, but we left the key in the ignition both at home and in town.

"Should we do any of those things today?" I asked them.

"No way," Molly said. "One time, a lady drove through our neighborhood in the daytime and grabbed every large toy she saw in the front yards, throwing them in the back of her van."

Yes, the question brought up all kinds of bad happenings in neighborhoods. We realized that our grandkids were not alone in longing for those times of the past. We wished for them back, too. As the discussion slowly fizzled out, we talked about the people we know personally: Good people. Trustworthy people. So, we decided the world wasn't all bad.

⤳ *DAY FOUR* ⤳

A SCARE

Allison

Well, I scared myself and everyone else this morning. I was feeling really low, and couldn't find my diabetes kit—it looks like a small purse—so I could test my blood sugar. We searched our bedroom—what a mess we made—and then the luggage in the hallway while Grandma checked around the house. I was feeling worse and worse from all the effort.

Oh, I hate diabetes!

Finally, Grandma took charge and told me to drink some juice. It was the logical thing to do because I always feel this way when my blood sugar is low, and I always need to drink juice to bring it back up. I was going to need my kit sooner or later, though, so we had to find it. Grandma wanted to know everywhere I'd been and everything I'd done since I last used it, and she sent someone off to look in those places. We weren't having any luck, and I was about to call Mom and Dad because they would know what I should do. Grandma said not to worry because it had to be around here somewhere unless it grew legs and walked off. Then Grandpa came in from the barn carrying my kit. He found it right where I had safely put it—on top of a corral post.

We all cheered and hollered, "Yay, Grandpa!" and hugged him. He hadn't known about the fussing that was going on but said he would take all the hugs he could get. All's well that ends well. Oh, now I'm starting to sound like Grandma.

Elliott

Today was so exciting! Caleb told me to bring my bug book along because he had a surprise up by the tractor shed. When we got there, we found several little mounds of dirt on the ground with tiny holes in the middle about the size of a pencil. Caleb knew they were antlion mounds or traps. We sat down and read all about how the larvae of the antlion digs the holes in a cone shape and then waits at the bottom. When an ant or other insects crawl in, the loose dirt traps them and dinner is served.

Charlie

I had a great morning exploring the creek and climbing trees with the guys. We took tin cans, plastic bottles, and other stuff we thought would float so we could have "boat" races down the stream. It was a blast!

However, this afternoon didn't start out so well. Josh and Caleb wanted to work on the barn loft some more. I hate hammering. Although Elliott is younger than me, he is better at it. Of course, Grandpa gave him a lighter hammer. I didn't want to give up or be a big baby, but it really hurts when I miss the nail. I thought I was getting the hang of it and then, bam! My poor thumb. It hurt so bad that I cried, threw down the hammer, and went to the house. Then I wasted the rest of a perfectly good vacation afternoon pouting and feeling sorry for myself.

Later that evening, when Molly and I were gathering eggs and feeding the chickens, she reminded me she had cried when she was not able to get off the swing at the creek. I know how scared Molly was because she isn't very good at such things, like I'm not very good at hammering. I guess I should give it another try.

Allison

Erin, Katie, and I were working in the kitchen doing the supper dishes and making brownies for tomorrow, and I asked Grandma if she thought all bad things that happen to us work for good. Katie had told me a Bible verse about that. Grandma said that the way we react to bad things makes a big difference. We talked about Molly's good attitude when she can't always do the things she wants to do.

What if she always pouted and complained? Or what if she was always angry about it? She wouldn't be happy, and we wouldn't like to be around her. It was a good lesson for me.

Then Grandma said, "I have a true story that fits your question. My mom—your great-grandmother, Edith—only went to school through the eighth grade because her mom—that would be your great-great-grandmother, Sarah—had shingles and was very sick. Mom needed to stay home and help with the work. She always felt disappointed that she couldn't finish school like the other girls her age.

"Much later in life, after marrying my father and having five boys and me, she realized something very important and told me about it one day. She said that if she hadn't stayed home and learned how to sew, cook, garden, preserve food, make sauerkraut and hominy, and many other important skills, she wouldn't have been able to take care of her big family through the Great Depression years. So, you see, something good did come out of her disappointment. It just took time for her to realize it."

We started thinking of sayings that fit and came up with: *behind every cloud is a silver lining, there's an upside to every downside*, and *there's no great loss without some small gain*.

"There's a light at the end of the tunnel," Grandpa added as he came in.

"Maybe not if it is nighttime," I said.

Then I hurried into the bedroom and typed Grandma's story as fast as I could because it was already time for our bedtime story.

Grandpa

Story time became question and answer time again. The grandkids wanted to know how and why we bought this farm. We thought they already knew we wanted to grow everything we could and do it organically, but as they explained themselves better, we realized they meant how did we choose this very one. So, I told the story.

FINDING THE FARM

Grandpa

We found our farm advertised on the internet, fell in love with it while looking at the photo of the small red barn, and then decided to see it for real. What got Grandma and me excited was the spring. Water is essential, and with the spring, we would always have it. Then we were overwhelmed by the diversity of the farm. You may have noticed that out in the cedar trees, it feels like you are hiking in the mountains of Colorado.

Josh, Katie, and Caleb agreed. That is where their other grandparents live.

We also liked the creek bordering one side of the farm where the area is still natural wilderness—a great place to explore.

They all nodded enthusiastically.

When we mow, we save a little strip along the fence for the birds and butterflies and still have enough pasture for a few animals and places for our gardens and orchards. Yes, it is a wonderful little paradise out here in the middle of nowhere, while still not that far from a highway and town. A perfect place for grandchildren to visit, don't you think?

"Yes, we've had great fun hiking and exploring," Erin said.

"Once, when we were in the creek," Katie said, "I slipped and fell in the mud!"

"Then I tried to help her," Charlie added, "but instead, I got my foot stuck, my shoe came off, and then I fell in the mud trying to put it back on. We had to be hosed off when we got back to the house."

We quietly left them chattering and went to bed. I was almost asleep when Grandma whispered, "They are going to have plenty of stories to tell their grandchildren someday."

Charlie

Grandma and the girls found an old song about hammering and sometimes play it when we come in. It has a very catchy tune, and it's hard to go to sleep when the words keep running through my head.

THE CISTERN

Katie

I often go with Grandpa to milk the cow. At first, we all took turns because Grandpa wanted everyone to have the experience. I like to do it and soon became his milking partner. The cow's name is Bessie. Not very original. She is gentle and never kicks at us. I guess she wants to be milked. Grandpa lets me do it until my hands and arms get tired and then he finishes. He can squirt milk a few feet, right into the barn cat's mouth. It is so funny to watch the cat jump to catch it. I've tried, but with no luck. The cat doesn't even try to catch it for me. He just turns his head and looks bored while waiting for Grandpa to take over. Sometimes it hurts my feelings and sometimes it makes me mad. Grandpa says that cats have a mind of their own.

Molly

We girls continue our "handiwork" as Grandma calls it. We do a little each day in-between our excursions. Allison and Erin are good at crocheting and are trying to get their scarves finished before we go home. Today, I noticed Grandma doing some mending on her sewing machine and I asked her if I could learn to sew. Grandma's eyes lit up as she said she would *love* to help me. She found some material scraps and let me practice simple seams. I caught on quickly, much to her delight. Then I saw her staring off into the distance and I thought, *I bet she is thinking about something special for me to sew tomorrow*.

Sophie

I'm doing okay on my crocheting. So far, I can do two stitches: a single and double crochet. They are pretty uneven, but I'm getting better each time I try. Grandma thinks I'm doing quite well for my age. My favorite is embroidering my pillow case. I want to have it finished when we leave. It will be so much fun to sleep on a pillow case I embroidered all by myself. Mommy will be so proud of me.

Josh

After our morning ride, Caleb and I asked Grandpa if we could help him with something. Well, there was a job that needed doing each summer that he hadn't gotten around to yet, and he said he would love the help.

We put three spades, three pails, a shovel, and two extra pairs of leather work gloves in the tractor bucket. Grandpa and Elliott rode the tractor up the hill to the northwest pasture. Caleb, Charlie, and I took a shortcut across the field on one of the deer trails. Grandpa stopped near the fence where an area was covered with prickly pear cactus plants. They are very neat, and I have seen them for sale in the city. I told Grandpa he had a fortune here. He wasn't interested. He mostly wants to keep them from spreading and is also trying to make the patch smaller and smaller each year. Prickly pear cactus is not good for animals.

We took turns digging out those which were coming up here and there, putting them in pails with a shovel, and then dumping them in the tractor bucket. Boy, did we have to be careful. Those needles can be treacherous, even through the leather gloves. Most of the work was too hard for Charlie and Elliott, but they were good at scouting them out for us. After we dug the strays, we started closing in on the patch. By then, the tractor bucket was heaping full and it was time to stop and take it to the burn pile. We were hot and tired anyway. Grandpa was happy and said the work went lots faster with many hands and was more fun with company.

Then we heard Elliott hollering for us to come and see what he discovered. Back under the trees was a large hole lined with cement with an opening in the top about the size of a manhole cover. It was an old cistern for holding water where a windmill once stood. Grandpa knew about it, but we hadn't seen it. He suggested we come back with a ladder and flashlight, and climb down and investigate. Elliott and Charlie weren't so sure. Hmmm. Actually, I wasn't sure, either, but I didn't say so.

After lunch, we went back to the cistern. Grandpa put the ladder down the hole and we looked in with his powerful flashlight. We couldn't believe what we saw. Mostly kid's stuff, at least on top. Caleb and I took turns going down and pushing one dirty thing after another up the ladder to Grandpa. There was a baby stroller, scooter, and a small training bike that took several tries before we got them up and out the hole. Then we brought up stuffed animals, toys, and all kinds of things that had gotten wet and ruined.

Grandpa just kept shaking his head and saying, "What kind of people would dump their belongings down there?" He had heard about a family who rented the place before my grandparents bought it. A neighbor had jokingly said that the sheriff's car was there about as often as the school bus.

The father must have gotten in trouble with the law because one day, the family left in a hurry, and evidently dumped the things they couldn't take with them in the cistern. We boys were quiet, thinking about children watching their daddy driving a load of their toys up the hill. I guess he didn't want anyone else playing with them either. What a mean man.

Grandpa started to say we should quit since the tractor bucket was getting full, when Caleb came flying up the ladder, yelling, "I'm not going back. There's a snake down there!"

Grandpa took the flashlight and started down. Sure enough, Caleb had uncovered a large bull snake. It was probably just as scared as Caleb. We wondered how it got down there. Maybe it fell out of the tree above the cistern. Most of all, we wondered if it could ever get out. We weren't about to help. Grandpa suggested we leave the ladder. Maybe it could crawl up it.

Charlie had a better idea. Since bull snakes can climb trees, he thought maybe a long branch would work. There were dead branches everywhere, so we searched for a long thick one, dragged it over, and stuck it down the hole. When we got back to the house, we raced for the shower and used lots of soap. What a day!

THE GRAND CANYON

Grandma

Tonight, I'm going to tell you a vacation adventure. It was Grandpa's idea, of course, that he and I should ride mules on the Bright Angel Trail going down 4,380 feet to the bottom of the Grand Canyon and Colorado River. Usually, you need to make arrangements a year in advance, but there was a cancellation during the hottest part of summer. We signed up and planned our vacation around that time. I know it sounds like a fun thing to do, but I am afraid of heights. I have looked off a small bridge over a stream in a park and become dizzy, so I was quite certain I couldn't look down into a deep, deep canyon while riding on a mule.

The evening we arrived, a guide welcomed us and showed a film of others taking the trail to the bottom so we would know what to expect. I learned something I could put my trust in: a mule had never fallen off. Then the guide took us to a lookout area over the canyon. I hung on to the low wall in front of me and became light-headed. Everything out there and down there seemed blurry. My head was spinning, and I was sure the trip would be impossible for me. Surprisingly, the guide, who was familiar with how people reacted when they looked over the side, said he could tell I would be able to do it.

That night as I lay in bed, I felt terrified while thinking about what might happen in the morning. I didn't want to back out at the last minute or embarrass Larry or myself. I also didn't want to faint and fall off the cliff. I thought of our children without a mother and asked Grandpa why we had to do such difficult things to have fun. He told me that if I didn't want to, we could just skip it. Yeah, as if I wanted to be the cause of *that* disappointment. I finally drifted off to sleep.

I always deal with heights better in the morning, so as we all gathered in the corral and mounted the mules, I was determined I would face my fears and not let Grandpa or myself down. I mustered all the courage I could find and repeated to myself that no mule had ever fallen off the cliff.

We lined up in single file. The wrangler told us to keep our mule close to the one in front of ours because if a mule noticed he was behind, he would take off and run to catch up. I decided my mule was going to have his nose next to the other's rear end the whole trip down. For some reason, Grandpa's mule didn't get behind mine, so he was farther back.

I didn't know it, but Grandpa was suddenly getting scared and having second thoughts. He knew we could change our mind and get our money back up to this point, but once your mule started down the steep trail, there was no turning back. Then he realized I had already started down. The first turn was terrifying! Soon after, I looked up at Grandpa. *Uh, oh!* He didn't wave or smile back.

The trail was often narrow, so my outside leg, which was hanging over the mule's wide belly, was actually over the side of the cliff. I never looked down at those times. Every now and then, we stopped. One time, it was my luck to be right at the sharp curve of a switchback. That meant my mule's head and neck were hanging over the edge until he was able to turn. I felt like I was suspended in space. I sat there slowly counting and telling myself to breathe. I knew I would be okay as long as I didn't faint and fall off the mule. Was I ever relieved when we started moving again.

We were required to wear long pants, long-sleeved shirts, hats, and bandanas to keep from breathing dust. I don't remember being unbearably hot. However, when we stopped at a little oasis called Indian Garden, where they gave each of us a boxed lunch, we were told to lie down in the spring until our clothes were soaked before starting down the trail again. The afternoon would be even hotter, and we certainly didn't want to have heat stroke.

I eventually became somewhat used to the heights and reminded myself to look at the incredible views. What unbelievable beauty!

The hikers had to take the same trail and were interesting to watch. Some were only going part way, but a few were headed for the bottom. If they saw our mule train coming, they needed to find a wider part of the trail so they could stand against the sheer wall of the canyon until we all passed. They weren't too happy if a mule did his business right beside them or let out big, long, noisy gas!

There was a large sign at the beginning of the trail and other signs along the way, warning hikers about what to wear and the amount of water they should be carrying. Over and over again, we saw people who had disregarded the important instructions and were in shorts, tank tops, and no hats. It worried me when I saw people, especially families, who were without water or only had small containers. Our wrangler told us they have to rescue such hikers every year.

When we reached the canyon floor, we came to Phantom Ranch, where we shared a nice cabin with a family of mice. I was tired, and my poor hips and legs hardly worked when I got off the mule. I decided to take a nap, but Grandpa listened to a park ranger tell stories about the area. In the evening, we went to the ranch house, where we were served a steak supper, and chatted and laughed with the others about our day. Then we took a short walk before crawling into our bunk beds. It was an interesting place that still had a few wild donkeys that had descended from those left by miners years before.

The next morning, we went up the South Kaibab Trail, which was much faster and had new scenery. When we made it to the top, it was a little sad leaving those with whom we had shared this unique experience. It seemed strange that we wouldn't see them again. I was happy, though, that I hadn't let my fear of heights win because I would have missed a wonderful adventure. Your Grandpa and I made a special memory together.

Allison said, "Grandma, we have taken some fun trips, also. I should write about them so I can tell my grandchildren someday."

KATIE'S HORSE

Molly

After morning chores, everyone planned to go on a long hike, following the creek as far as time would allow. I would need to skip this outing. Sophie didn't want to leave me behind. She even volunteered to stay, but I told her that I didn't mind since I was going to practice on the sewing machine.

As I expected, Grandma had an easy project ready. She had searched through her patterns until she found one for a simple apron that ties around the waist. Then we went through her material stash until I found a piece I liked. We even found some rickrack to trim the pocket. This was the first time I ever pinned a pattern on material and cut out something. Then I began to sew. Grandma said I was a natural.

It took all morning but I was just finishing when I heard everyone out at the hydrant cleaning up. Sophie was the first to run in and see how I was doing. She squealed excitedly as she bragged about my apron. Then she modeled it for everyone as if she was strutting down a runway.

Caleb

This afternoon, Josh and I were out by the lane talking to Grandpa about a small dead tree he wanted to take down. We know quite a bit about sawing a wedge out of a tree so it will fall in the right place. We learned this from working with our other grandpa who lives in the mountains of Colorado. I was telling Grandpa we should do it because the cleanup would be fast and easy with all the extra hands.

Suddenly, we heard quite a racket. One of the horses was racing down the lane toward us without a rider.

"Oh, no!" Grandpa said. He had quite a look of concern on his face.

As we started after the horse, we saw the girls across the field.

Allison and Erin were riding double, as Erin had given Katie her horse. "The best thing to do when you get thrown off a horse is to get right back on," she had told Katie.

As the story was told by the three girls—mostly at the same time—they had gone riding across the road and into the neighbor's field, with permission, of course. They were crossing a small ditch when a vulture flew up from the ground and spooked Katie's horse. He bucked her off, continued bucking wildly, and then took off for home. Thankfully, there weren't any cars coming when he crossed the road. Katie was only bruised, but still hurting and flustered.

Katie

I got bucked off a horse today, and now I don't feel like I can trust them. Erin says to just keep riding and I will get over it. She also explained that as I become a better rider, I can learn to hold tight with my legs, calm the horse, and possibly not be thrown. I doubt that I'll ever have a chance to become that good but maybe. I'm hurting a little, so I decided to stay in the house, rest, and do girl stuff. My embroidering is coming along nicely, and I learned how to make French knots for the center of the flowers, and loop stitches for the petals.

Elliott

I kept feeling like crying today. Grandma noticed, and after asking me a lot of questions, she came to the conclusion that I was sick. Homesick, that is. She wondered if maybe a nice long phone call to Mommy and Daddy tonight might help.

They volunteered to come and get me, and Grandpa said he could meet them halfway. Then, after telling them everything I'd been doing, I realized I didn't want to go home and miss the fun. I would feel sad later when I listened to everyone's exciting stories. Mommy said I could call every night if I wanted to. Then Daddy asked to speak to Charlie and Sophie. After the call, Sophie gave me a big hug, and Charlie asked me if I wanted to sleep beside him.

MOOSE

Grandma

Tonight's vacation story is a moose adventure. Yes, a moose adventure! Your Grandpa and I were in the third week of our vacation to the Northeast, and he wanted to go to the very end of Nova Scotia, Canada, to Cape Breton Highlands National Park. He had read about the moose living in their national park and wanted to see one. The scenery along the way was so beautiful. The campsite was nice, and we slept well in the cool weather.

We arrived at the first trailhead a little later in the morning than we had hoped. Choosing three of the twenty-eight trails that sounded promising, we hiked the two shorter ones before lunch. The surroundings were special. We saw moose tracks and droppings but no moose. We knew we should have been out at dawn and were disappointed. We decided to have a leisurely afternoon and take the third and longer trail at dusk.

It was time to head to town for lunch, and as we rounded a curve in our car, there stood a massive dark brown moose right in front of us, filling up our lane. A bull moose with a huge rack! He glanced at us, stepped over the guard rail, and disappeared into the thick foliage. Well, we had searched and searched the forest the whole morning, and then he just walked across the road in front of our car.

We started the 4.3-mile Skyline Trail Loop at about 6:00 p.m. that evening. Yes, we were starting as the other people were coming back, but were prepared with water, a flashlight, and toilet paper. Another couple started soon after us. They were young, and as they overtook us, we said, "Yell if you see a moose!" They did. A moose crossed the path right in front of them. We caught up and watched him roaming and grazing through the trees.

We reached the headland where there were boardwalks for paths and a $2,000 fine for stepping off them. This kept people from ruining the area. What a beautiful view of the mountains and ocean! It was one of the prettiest places we've ever been and worth the trip, even if we hadn't seen a moose.

We still wanted to continue the loop, although it was getting late. The path was mostly single file with a little clearing on each side, and then chest-high ferns. It felt like the forest was closing in on us. We knew moose were in there when we came to a patch of white birch trees that had been stripped of leaves and branches as high as the moose could reach, leaving a thick umbrella of green above. A few yards farther, we saw another patch, and there stood a bull moose! We watched him for several minutes as he grazed toward us. The first time I looked through the binoculars, he took a couple of steps toward me and I almost ran. It was such a relief to take the binoculars down and realize he wasn't that close.

We wondered how we were going to continue with him coming toward us. As we tiptoed on past, both of us kept looking back to see if he was following. Grandpa was right behind me and we had hardly gotten started when we rounded a little curve in the narrow trail. I stopped dead in my tracks, and Grandpa bumped right into me. A moose was lying in the grass in a small opening touching the trail. I lost his image for a moment, but then the outline of his massive rack reappeared. I think all the blood had drained from my head.

"Oh, my goodness! Oh, my goodness!" I whispered. My knees about buckled. He was huge. He got up and limped a couple of steps onto our path. He just stood there. I started looking for a way of escape and noticed Grandpa doing the same. We had read that we should circle around, but we were boxed in between two bull moose and decided to wait. He was taking his sweet time foraging, though, and it was getting darker. His ears weren't flat (agitated) or flat with his head down (very agitated), but listening to him snort was still unnerving.

The good thing about waiting so long for him to get out of the way was that we got a good look at a moose. A very good look! Finally, we were able to continue. That was so scary and so exciting at the same time! What an experience!

Then I got exasperated with Grandpa. It was fairly dark and we had a long way to go. As I hurried down the trail, I turned around and he wasn't following me. He had noticed he could get a photo of a moose in a partially lit sky in a clearing. I hollered for him. Finally, he came. I told him if it was all right with him, I didn't care if I saw another moose. Ever! We needed to keep moving. Well, we hadn't gone more than a few yards when we came around a curve and there stood another bull moose grazing off to the side.

We were power walking in the near dark with our eyes on the rugged path so we wouldn't fall. "When are we going to finish this loop and be back on the wider trail?" I continued to ask.

Grandpa reminded me that he had never been on this path before either, and not to break an ankle.

Before long, we saw a cow moose but stopped only long enough to take a quick look at her through the binoculars. She was looking right back. If she had a baby, she might have been dangerous, so we continued on.

I walked a lot back then and knew we were moving fast. Grandpa shined the flashlight in front of us so we wouldn't stumble over the rocks. I felt like Hansel and Gretel, and the song on the kids' old story record ran repeatedly through my mind.

We were so relieved when we were back on the main, wide, smoother path. We had walked the last half hour in complete darkness with our heads down. If a moose had been standing there, we probably would have walked smack into him.

When we finally got back to where we had started, there were our young friends with their car headlights shining down the path. They didn't know we had a flashlight and were worried about us. It was so nice of them. The four of us were very excited and couldn't believe how close we had been to so many moose. We stood there and told our stories for several minutes.

This was such an exciting adventure. As we lay in our tent, unable to fall sleep, I wondered aloud what our children would think about us taking such risks. Grandpa thought we should call and tell them to sell the house because we were not coming home. Ha!

"I hope I get to go on as many adventures as you and Grandpa when I grow up," Sophie said.

"I think being at this farm is an adventure," Molly said.

A MYSTERY PHONE CALL

Erin

It began raining last night, which made everyone happy because it is so dry and dusty. But then it rained most of today and it started getting old. Actually, it poured. Grandma described it as coming down in sheets. Grandpa said it was a real gully washer.

We played some longer games such as Monopoly and King Oil, since there was plenty of time. We girls also worked on our projects and helped bake cookies. Boy, we sure go through the cookies.

Both Charlie and Elliott were rather quiet and I could tell they were a little frightened because of the lightning and large claps of thunder. Also, the electricity was out for a while. When it finally stopped raining by late afternoon, we had gotten 5.5 inches. According to the news, other nearby places received even more, which washed out a small bridge and did other damage.

We let the animals out, and then Grandpa and Grandma walked down to the creek with us. We couldn't get close because the banks were overflowing with rushing water and the swing was floating. Grandma didn't feel it was safe for so many kids running here and there and shooed us back to the house with instructions that we were not to go near the creek until Grandpa gave us permission. We played around the barn and house yard and were as happy as the animals to run about in the clean, fresh air.

Charlie

We had to stay in today because of the rain. The thunder and lightning and howling wind were exciting but also scary. Poor Elliott was looking wide-eyed and sad again, and I couldn't seem to cheer him. I guess two weeks away from Mom and Dad are too much for a six-year-old. Funny thing is, I'm starting to feel that way, too, even though I'm usually having lots of fun. Maybe it's the rain.

A strange thing happened while we were eating supper. Grandpa got a phone call, and he lit up with a huge smile. Grandma seemed to know what it was about, even though Grandpa didn't say more than, "Uh huh . . . sure . . . I'll see you later tomorrow morning, then . . . bye."

"Just in the nick of time," Grandma said when he got off the phone. Whatever that meant.

Allison

We had story time again before going to bed. The storm reminded Grandma of a true story of her childhood she thinks our family should remember, so I am trying to get every word written down. No one talked during the story, but afterward, there were lots of questions. I'm glad I'll be able to say I heard the tornado story straight from Grandma's mouth.

THE TORNADO

Grandma

When I was a very little girl, a tornado struck our Iowa farm. It came quickly, and the cave was too far from the house for us to get to in time. As the strong winds hit, the glass from the door where my brother Stanley stood watching, blew out and cut his forehead. Mom rushed him, my other brother Frank, and me to the basement where they tried to hold the outside basement door shut.

You can imagine how frightening it must have been to hear all the terrible noise going on outside and not knowing if we were going to be blown away. Actually, I don't remember that at all. I only have two memories of the tornado. One would think the frightful noise would be one of them, but my first memory is when it was over and we went upstairs. Some of the windows had blown out, and the dishes on the table were broken and scattered on the floor. Mom told my brother to carry me over to a chair so I wouldn't cut my bare feet on the glass. Next, my mother and brothers must have looked outside.

I'm going to skip ahead, now, and tell one of my older brother's account of the tornado that I learned just a few years ago. I have five older brothers, and this one, Dick, was working for another farmer that day. He came into our little town of Washta, Iowa where my dad picked him up to bring him home. Our farm was only a mile and a half from town, but the rain was coming down so hard they could barely see the road in front of them. As they were inching along, suddenly, there was a terrific flash of lightning that lit up the whole countryside for a moment.

"Dad, the farm isn't there," Dick said.

"Oh, we just haven't gotten that far," my dad replied.

Then, there was another flash of lightning, and guess what? The farm was gone. There weren't any buildings—only the small white house sitting all by itself and safely holding my mom, my two brothers, and me.

My next memory is when all the people came to our farm to see the destruction. I remember lots of men roaming around outside, and the women sitting around on chairs inside. I suppose I remember the women because they probably were paying a lot of attention to me. After all, I was just a little thing. Probably as cute as a bug!

You've seen on television what a tornado can do, so you can imagine a huge barn, a double corn crib, A-houses for pigs, a chicken and brooder house, and other buildings flattened or totally gone. My mother had recently brought home 500 baby chickens, and they and the egg-laying hens were scattered dead all over the yard. A horse had been picked up and deposited in another field, unhurt but he was a little crazy for a while.

Do you wonder why all the other buildings, large and small, were taken, but our little house was still there? I do, too, although I never gave it a thought when I was a child, and I was never afraid of storms. I find this curious. I'm guessing that since my mother never acted like she was afraid, I wasn't, either. Also, my father would stand out on the steps on one side of the house or the other and watch the sky when a storm was coming. I always trusted that—way more than I trust listening to the forecast and sirens blowing.

I was too little to remember the cleanup, or much of the rebuilding. I suppose the broken lumber that couldn't be reused was burned. I do remember when the tiles from the silo were later used to build the chicken house for the egg-laying hens. It was a great chicken house, and it was my job to gather eggs when I was older. We have driven past the farm recently, and that sturdy chicken house is still there.

During my whole time growing up, we had two piles of junk out in the barnyard. Whenever another piece of wood or metal resurfaced from the ground, it was thrown on one of those piles. My brother, Frank, had a unique way of finding the nails—in his feet. Our small-town doctor got so upset with him for going barefoot, that he informed him the next time he stepped on a nail, he wasn't going to take care of him.

Recently, my sister-in-law told me she was young and still living with her parents at the time of the tornado and she remembers how they found out about it. Back then, the phones were on what they called shared party lines, and if there was a disaster, everyone heard three long rings. She only recalls hearing the three long rings twice in her life: when President Roosevelt declared war on Germany and after our tornado.

"Oh, that must have been really scary," Elliott said.

"I feel so sorry for our great-grandpa losing all his farm buildings," Joshua said.

"And all Great-Grandma's chickens," Erin added.

PART THREE

THE SECOND WEEK

A SURPRISE

Elliott

Everyone was sad when Allison said our vacation was half over. I was also homesick. Grandma said so. Then, Grandpa told me I should skip riding with Sophie and Molly after chores because he wanted me to go with him on an errand. He didn't say why he chose me. On the way, Grandpa told me stories and I talked about the things we kids had been doing as we explored. I kept waiting, but not once did Grandpa hint at where we were going. I didn't ask since it seemed to be a secret. Wherever it was, it sure made Grandpa's face look happy.

After a long time, we turned into a lane leading up to a large farmhouse. A man and his son came out and greeted us. Then they took us out to the barn where seven little puppies were yipping and wrestling with each other. When they saw us, they all started jumping up on the side of their box, like, "Pick *me!* Pick *me!*" Grandpa had already chosen the puppy he wanted and paid for her. He had been waiting until the mother weaned them. She was a little yellow lab and so soft and sweet.

Grandpa picked her up and called her "Dolly." She wiggled all over and licked his whole face, even his mouth. *"Phlettt!"* Grandpa didn't seem to mind that much. We stayed a while and watched the puppies play. They were so fun.

I got to hold Dolly all the way home. At first, she was pretty wild, taking turns licking me and trying to crawl all over me. Before long, she wore herself out and fell asleep on my lap. Grandpa said he had a small kennel out in the shed to put in the mudroom for Dolly to sleep in, and Grandma had the needed supplies. I couldn't wait to get back and show the new puppy to the others. I remembered to thank Grandpa for taking me along. He said he thought I could use a little cheering up. Dolly did exactly that.

When we reached home, Grandpa said, "I think we broke one of Grandma's rules. We're late for lunch."

Katie

Grandpa and Elliott went for a drive this morning and brought home a puppy. Her name is Dolly and she is adorable. Everyone wanted to hold her at the same time, so we sat in a circle out in the grass and put her in the middle. She was so excited and ran from one of us to the other, sniffing us all and trying to chew on our shoes. Then she plopped down and went to sleep just like a baby.

Grandma

When it was story time tonight, I thought about the baby fawn Grandpa and I watched through our binoculars this spring and decided to tell the grandkids about my childhood pet.

JUDY

Grandma

My Dad—your great-grandfather Charley Moore—allowed people to pass through our Iowa farm to fish in the Little Sioux River, but never to hunt. That was a curious thing because the deer ate a fair amount of his corn crop. Back in his day, it was normal for farmers to leave some land for the birds and wild animals, and his river bottom land was perfect for deer.

On the day my story begins, he was cultivating down in the field closest to the river when he noticed the edge of the cultivator was about to run over a baby deer. He couldn't stop in time and jumped off the tractor to see if she was hurt. Luckily, the fawn was only a few days old and wasn't touched in her indented nest. Dad picked her up and brought her home. This was so out of character for him, but I suppose he couldn't leave her out in the field where he was about to plant a corn crop. Actually, I'm not sure what he thought, but much to our delight, she became ours and we named her Judy.

That was many years ago, but one of my funniest memories of Judy is when she awoke from her nap that first day and tried to walk on our linoleum floor. Her long sticklike legs slid straight out to the sides like we've seen Bambi's do in the movies. That had us rolling in laughter! It was like watching a cartoon.

My brother, Frank, and I took turns bottle feeding her. As she grew, we taught her how to jump over the clothesline by first lowering it as far as it would go and then gradually raising it. Of course, deer are natural jumpers and she didn't need to be taught, but we had so much fun playing with her.

Dad shut Judy in a shed at night for her protection. Then the game warden learned about her. He came to visit one day and told us it was against the law to enclose her. We had to do what he said, so we left the door propped open. Judy was tame by then and went in on her own at nighttime. Our dog, Jack, would protect her from any wild animals if necessary.

The game warden came back twice and took her to both the county and the state fairs where children could see a young deer up close and reach through the fence to pet her.

Judy also became quite popular in our small town of Washta, Iowa, which was only one and a half miles from our farm. Both Jack and Judy, who had become great pals, would take off and visit the children on the school playground. One time, I was at my friend's house when her mother was showing home movies. Surprise! There on the screen was Judy eating their garden.

When Judy grew older, she would disappear at times. Then, I might be out doing my chicken chores, and she would suddenly be standing there watching me with her soft, large eyes. Of course, we were happy to see each other, and she would come to me and rear up on her hind legs like she did when she was little. I was just a young girl and her hooves were sharp. She had become more than I could manage, and I was afraid of her.

One day, we realized Judy hadn't come back for quite some time. That was so sad, but we hoped she had found a mate and might someday have her own baby down by our river. Not in the middle of the field, of course.

"Grandma, I bet you are the only person in the whole world to have a deer for a pet!" Katie said.

"Well, I'm the only person I know of," I replied. "It is one of my happiest childhood memories.

Josh

We all loved Grandma's story and thought it would be fun to walk through the forested part of the farm in the spring and search for fawns. Who knows what else we might find. Grandma always tells us to practice a little wonder while we are out there.

"Look for some magic," she says.

Allison

Dolly is supposed to be sleeping in her kennel on the porch, but she is missing her mommy and the other puppies and is whimpering and yelping. Grandpa is such a softy. When I was doing my bedtime diabetes test, I saw him get the kennel and move it into their bedroom. I bet Dolly gets to sleep in bed with them tonight.

JACK THE ROOSTER
AND THE HAMMERING FEVER

Sophie

I got so mad! Jack chases me every time he sees me. I hate that rooster. He picks on me and Elliott the most. Grandpa thinks it is because we are the shortest. I leave a long stick by the steps and take it with me each time I go out toward the chicken yard. I call it *the Jack stick*. This morning, I forgot it and the chickens were free ranging all over the place. As soon as he saw me, he took off straight in my direction. I threw my shoes at him and screamed and screamed until Joshua came to my rescue.

Oh, that rooster made me so mad!

Josh

We finished the floor in the barn loft yesterday, and this afternoon, a neighbor came by with a truckload of hay and straw bales. These were the rectangular ones that could be lifted by Grandpa's hay trolley and taken across the loft and dropped. The straw will be used for bedding for the animals, and the hay for their food.

We were neatly stacking the bales when we decided that making forts, tunnels, and playing tag seemed more fun. Grandpa just laughed and gave up. It was a blast but before long, we began itching all over in the heat and headed for the water hydrant. Then a great water fight began. Maybe we should only play in the loft after evening chores and just before showers. We'll ask the girls to join us.

Caleb

Now that the loft floor is finished, Josh and I have the hammering fever. We want to build something. The loft needs a better ladder or steps, but Grandpa said we should save that until another summer when we are older. A treehouse. Yes, we could build a treehouse, but our time is running out.

Grandma had an idea, though. She wants a deer stand, or little platform in a tree down by the spring where she can wait quietly in the twilight and watch the deer come to drink. There are hoof prints upon hoof prints around there, and she wants to count and see how many deer come each evening. She thinks it would be fun to watch them and maybe get a photo or two.

Grandpa teased her and told her it would be easier to set up a game camera. Anyway, tomorrow, we are going to scout out the perfect tree, then load the tractor up with old lumber and get started. I thought a couple of us could sit up there one night before we leave.

"How long can you be quiet?" Grandpa asked me with a smile.

Grandma

I had to laugh when Sophie told us about Jack at supper. Her face turned red and she got mad all over again. So, for story time, I've decided to talk about my encounters with mean roosters.

THE MEAN ROOSTER

Grandma

When I was a girl about Allison's age, I often heard interesting stories about mean roosters chasing people. Sometimes I wished we had one of those wild roosters to add a little excitement around the farm. Then, one summer, we did. In fact, we had three. The minute they saw me coming out the kitchen door, they gave chase, and I soon found out it wasn't exciting after all.

I was told not to run, but instead to show the roosters who was boss. I tried, but they already knew who was boss, and it wasn't me. I could stand up to a huge cow, but not the roosters. Finally, I taught two of them to leave me alone, but not the third. I must have been his entertainment each day as he planned a new place to wait in hiding. Mom and Dad were full of instructions. It seemed to me I was more at fault for not being tough enough. It wasn't fair.

One day, Dad was waiting for me in the pickup truck. As I started across the yard, the mean rooster gave chase. I ran as fast as I could and jumped on the running board. Clinging to the door, I half turned and kicked as hard as I could. By luck, I connected with the rooster and hit him with such force that he flipped over backward and was knocked loony. When he finally got up, he slowly staggered off.

Dad laughed and laughed! I was pretty shaken, but would have really enjoyed the moment if I had known right then that I had finally won the battle. That rooster never chased me again. It was always fun to hear Dad tell others about it, and this time, it was *my* exciting rooster story.

"I think Jack will always win," Sophie said. "Grandma, could we eat him for Sunday dinner?"

BOBCATS AND RATTLESNAKES

Josh

We boys were excited this morning and hurried through our chores before breakfast so we could get down to the spring and find a place to build Grandma's deer stand.

"Let's get cracking," Grandpa said.

That is one of my favorite sayings of his. It just cracks me up! Anyway, we were ready to leave when Molly and Sophie came running in and hollering for Grandpa. Something was trying to get into the chicken pen.

Grandpa grabbed his rifle and headed out. It was a bobcat, and we could see two more at the edge of the

cedar trees. He shot up in the air and the bobcats took off. He followed, shooting in the air a couple times until he was sure they were far away. Grandpa said the chickens should stay in the pen today, although he didn't think the bobcats would return. Then he asked us if we all knew what to do if we encountered one.

"Appear bigger," we said.

"Wave our hands high above our head."

"Take off our shirt and hold it high above our head."

Elliott decided he could never appear big enough and he was going to stay in the house and play with Dolly. All of us giggled. Grandpa talked him into going with us to the spring by promising to bring the rifle. I thought it was interesting that we hadn't even left the yard this morning, but we all had one of those adventures Grandma talks about.

Erin

The boys went to the spring with Grandpa, and Molly and Sophie went riding. While waiting to use the horses, Katie made a chocolate cake, I hung two baskets of clothes on the clothesline, and Allison and Grandma picked green beans. Then we helped clean and cut the beans so Grandma could freeze them in bags for winter.

When it was our turn to ride, Grandma gave us permission to pack a lunch and water bottles to take on our longest horse ride yet. We turned the opposite direction on the road than we usually go, rode lazily up the hill, and had only gone about two miles when Katie's horse snorted and pricked up its ears. I could see on Katie's face that she thought, *Oh no, here I go again*.

We stopped immediately and looked around. I was the first to spot a snake up ahead. It looked like a rattlesnake sunning itself along the edge of the road. We headed back at a gallop and got Grandpa who had just driven up from the spring to get more lumber. He grabbed his rifle off the tractor and we squeezed into the truck beside him. I could tell that Grandpa was proud of us for noting landmarks so we could remember where we had spotted the snake.

He stopped far enough from the snake so as not to scare it and told us to stay put. We couldn't see from the truck if it was still there, but then we heard a loud crack as Grandpa shot it dead. He brought it back and threw it in the truck bed. Wow! It was a big one. As soon as we got back, I ran into the house and grabbed a tape measure. It was almost three and a half feet. Grandpa cut off the rattles for anyone who wanted one. Allison has always been the snake lover, so she was the first to take one.

The boys came walking back through the trees. They were wondering what the rifle shot was all about and why Grandpa hadn't come back. Needless to say, Elliott was pretty pale and wide-eyed. He took one look at the snake and said, "I only like bugs!" Poor Elliott. He may stay in the house and become Grandma's helper until it is time to go home. We gave up on our long horse ride and ate our lunch with everyone else. Maybe tomorrow.

Charlie

We went back to the spring this afternoon, but after Grandpa helped build the frame for the deer stand, there wasn't enough room for more than two people to be working at a time. While we were looking at all the deer tracks, Grandpa got the idea that Elliott and I might like to learn to track. He told Elliott that he was always looking at the ground for bugs anyway!

Elliott nervously reminded Grandpa to bring the rifle.

Grandpa thought that starting with something big and obvious might be a good idea, so we went up the hill to the chicken house and looked for bobcat tracks. They were easy to find in the soft dirt, but then we lost them in the trees. We memorized how they looked, though, and will recognize them if a bobcat comes around again. Along the game trails and creek where the animals come for water were also good places to look. I'm keeping a list of all the animal tracks I learn about while I'm here. So far, I have deer, bobcat, coyote, turkey, and pheasant.

Grandpa pointed out that if we learn the different tracks, we can be aware of any predator that might harm us or the livestock.

Grandpa

What a day! Since a glimpse of the three bobcats was so exciting to the grandkids this morning, I decided to tell them about my mountain lion encounter. Even though it happened several years ago, I still get shivers each time I tell the story.

THE MOUNTAIN LION

Grandpa

Grandma and I were on vacation and camping for the night at Ainsworth State Park in Oregon. Our tent was in a cozy site on the outer edge of the campground. It was a perfect place all snuggled under large evergreen trees and right next to a paved path leading to the bathhouse. If you aren't familiar with campground bathhouses, they are large buildings with men's facilities on one side and women's on the other.

We usually walk to the bathhouse together, but that morning, Grandma said I should go ahead since she was waking up slowly and was still getting dressed. I went in the first door to use the bathroom, and as I opened it to go out and take a few steps to the shower room, there stood a mountain lion less than twenty feet in front of me. He was a magnificent animal, full grown, and swishing his long tail while looking straight at me.

I was shocked but not afraid, for two reasons: he wasn't moving or growling, and I could have taken a step backward and the heavy door would have swung closed on its own. I was only in the bathroom about two minutes, and in hindsight, I wonder if he followed me up the path or watched me as I went in. A scary thought. Grandma thinks he must have already had breakfast!

All of a sudden, he turned and started down the path I had just come up. *Oh, no! Grandma might be coming up the path now. What should I do?* I ended up following him.

There he stood at the bottom of the path with his eyes

locked on our tent. He was listening to the noise Grandma was making on the nylon sleeping bag as she was trying to find the earing she'd dropped. If she came crawling out, she would look like prey to the big cat. So, I waved my hands and said, "Shoo!" Like shooing a chicken. He could have attacked, but he just ignored me and kept his eyes on the tent.

This next part of the story is where Grandma said I was a little crazy. She said I should have gotten into the car to be safe and then honked the horn to scare him away. But the mountain lion was ignoring me, so I thought I would go wide around him intending to get the camera out of the back seat of the car and take his picture. I took a couple steps and it seemed to spook him. With two leaps, he was into the brush and gone.

I hollered, "Mary, there was a mountain lion out here!"

"Oh, Larry, it was probably just a dog," she said.

I haven't let her forget those words. She never got to see him, but she heard the noise when he leaped into the brush.

We reported it to the park worker, and the area was roped off so park officials could later search for tracks. This lady had worked at the park part-time for ten years and never seen a mountain lion. I stayed overnight and saw one face to face.

"That story is a lot scarier than our seeing a bobcat and a rattlesnake," Katie said.

"I'm wondering about something, Grandpa," Elliott said. "Some of your stories are very scary. Doesn't anything ever get you or anything bad ever happen to you and Grandma?"

"Well, Elliott, we're still here, aren't we?" I answered as I laughed a little.

LOSING TRACK OF TIME

Grandma

Grandpa woke up last night thinking he heard Dolly whimpering to go outside. When he reached for her kennel door in the dark, he found it already open. He followed the sound down the hall, and found the puppy in the boys' room all snuggled up beside Elliott. I guess someone besides Dolly needed comforting during the night.

Erin

At breakfast, Grandma said they had run out of stories, so we should be prepared to participate in a discussion before bedtime tonight. She wanted each one of us to talk about some magic or miracle we discovered while here at the farm. She said that a miracle could be described as something unbelievable to us. Also, we might take turns telling what we've enjoyed the most at the farm so far.

We were a little quieter than usual as we left the house thinking about what we would say, but after chores, we started having fun and forgot. It was one of those special days when we all took our free time together and waded and played in the creek.

The boys pulled large dried weeds on the way and used them as spears, throwing them into the soft creek bank. Then they thought it great fun trying to catch minnows with their bare hands, throw rocks at floating tin cans, and race things downstream. Elliot was more fascinated with the water bugs and dragonflies. Charlie began searching the banks for animal tracks and found a mudslide. Josh thought it was probably a muskrat slide, so we all got excited and searched the banks at water level on both sides for muskrat dens.

We girls had just as much fun as the boys by just watching what the boys did. It was nice and cool in the water with the trees stretching out above us.

Probably the most fun was when we all climbed a huge, sprawling cottonwood. We each had our own branch for home base and played all sorts of games. We helped Molly up onto the lowest branch. Allison, who doesn't like heights, took the next lowest. She soon forgot about being scared, though, and played the games with us. Charlie chose the highest branch, of course. Sometimes he got out a little far and swayed in the wind. He loved the feel of it, but I worried and asked him to move closer to the trunk. He scowled a little but did it without complaining.

All of a sudden, Elliott announced he was hungry. We've all learned he gets really crabby when he's hungry. Then Allison realized her blood sugar must be low, and she was looking droopy. She needed a juice box—like, now! We had no idea what time it was, but climbed down the tree and up the bank so we could hurry back where we left our things. Josh ran ahead and retrieved Allison's kit and brought it back to her.

Well, our watches were safe and dry in our bags where we left them, but it was almost 1:00 p.m. and we still had to walk home and hose off. *Uh, oh. We broke one of Grandma's free-time rules.* We were late for lunch. Really late. We decided that Allison and Molly should stay and we would ask Grandpa to drive down and pick them up.

Grandpa and Grandma weren't mad but rather happy to see we were okay. Grandpa said it is complete freedom when you're having so much fun you lose track of time. I hadn't thought of it that way but knew it was a morning with my cousins I would always remember.

Elliott

I heard Grandpa tell Grandma he needed to get his chainsaw blades sharpened this afternoon. He was going to take the recyclables and go into town. He could also get her any needed groceries while he waited. I asked if I could go along because ever since I went with Grandpa to get Dolly, we have been pals.

I like talking to Grandpa. Today, he told me how he and Grandma try to reuse and recycle. Also, they don't use any chemicals on the farmland, so everything they grow is organic. I told him I know Mommy always buys organic because I go to the grocery store and the farmer's market with her. We pick up grass-fed beef at the mall parking lot on Saturday mornings, and she doesn't use chemicals to clean with. Grandpa said he is real proud of her.

When we were at the recycling place, Grandpa asked about the next date when all the farmers could bring in old tires, batteries, and used oil. He wants to get rid of a big tractor tire that wore out. I'm real proud of Grandpa, too, because he tries to take good care of his land.

Grandma

I asked the grandkids during supper if they had thought about their favorite thing about being here, and something miraculous, magical, or unbelievable to tell us about at story time. I could tell by their faces they had forgotten and the wheels in their heads were turning as they ate. They did a good job, though, and Grandpa and I found their choices interesting.

MIRACLES, MAGIC, AND FAVORITE THINGS: THE COUSINS

Elliott

I think the many different colors and patterns of dragonflies and butterflies are magical. I like Dolly the best. And cookies!

Charlie

My favorite thing is climbing trees, and I think the large cottonwood trees are miracles. I remembered to smell like you suggested, Grandma, and I thought about all the different things I've smelled on the farm. I like the barnyard smell the best because it makes me think of horses and playing in the hay loft.

Sophie

I find it unbelievable that a big horse will obey a little girl like me. My favorite thing is being with my cousins.

Molly

My favorite things to do are swinging over the creek, gathering eggs, and using the sewing machine. I found it mind-blowing how high the creek got after the storm and how fast the water was moving.

Erin

My favorite thing to do is to go horseback riding in the fields. We don't always talk. Sometimes we just listen to the sounds around us. I find it a miracle to see how many different kinds of birds there are. I like hearing their special songs. My friend Johanna is a birder, and I'm thinking that going bird watching might be a fun hobby.

Katie

I liked helping Grandpa milk the cow. He said I was the best milker of us all. I guess I ended up being the only milker of us all. I find all of nature to be a miracle.

Caleb

I liked to build. I hope we can come back and build a big tree house up in a cottonwood tree. After our day at the cistern, I've been thinking about our parents. I find it unbelievable that all of us have such good moms and dads.

Josh

I like helping Grandpa figure out how to do things, how to fix up the old buildings. Caleb and I are hoping we can come back next summer and help do some of the projects we talked about, such as building steps leading up to the loft and a new gate for Grandma's garden. I also like taking down dead trees. I find it a mystery how a newborn deer has no scent so that wild animals won't find its nest while the mother is out foraging.

Allison

I find all wildlife to be miracles, so I enjoyed the encounters with the bobcats and the rattlesnake. And I liked watching the deer and wild turkeys. My favorite thing is Grandpa and Grandma's stories. I want to write a book about it all someday.

SHENANIGAN DAY

Josh

I saw Caleb and Katie outside whispering together last night and figured there would soon be some mischief. I remembered Dad's words to the twins when we were dropped off: "No shenanigans!" Obviously, they didn't remember. It was like they couldn't contain themselves any longer and the orneriness spilled out of them the whole day long.

They have learned not to do something hurtful and not to pick on the same person twice, but they still pulled out all the tricks they could remember. Most had been practiced on me! I think they played their meanest prank on Grandma when Caleb unplugged the washing machine while it was washing a load of dirty jeans. Grandma tried everything and finally decided it was broken.

"What am I going to do with all these dirty clothes," she fretted, and headed out to get Grandpa.

I felt sorry for her. In the meantime, Katie reached behind the machine and plugged it back in. When Grandpa came in to check it out, the machine was working again as if nothing had happened.

Allison

Katie told me I had a booger on my nose right at the breakfast table. Embarrassing! I tried to get it with a napkin, but she kept saying I missed it, so I hurried to the bathroom mirror. No booger. I had been tricked.

Erin

Caleb called me outside while I was washing the breakfast dishes and then seemed to forget why. It was strange, but I soon found out the reason. While I was out there, Katie quickly taped the sprayer handle in the squeeze position, so when I turned on the faucet to rinse the dishes, I got sprayed right in the face. The whole front of my shirt was pretty much drenched. Everyone thought it so funny! It was a good joke, and I'm going to remember to do it to Mom. In the meantime, it is get-even time.

Elliott

There was a toad in the toe of my shoe this morning. I almost squished it when I shoved my foot in. It was an awful feeling, and I bet the toad didn't like it either. Someone had to put it in there since my shoes were in the mudroom. Hmmm? I'm going to give my shoes a whack from now on.

Molly

Caleb was hollering like crazy in the boy's bedroom. When Sophie and I rushed in, he clapped a fly in his hands.

"This fly was trying to buzz in my ear," he said. Then he quickly flashed a hand that was holding a smooshed fly, turned his hand over, looked at it for a couple seconds, and popped it into his mouth.

I thought I was going to puke.

He laughed. "Got ya! It was only a squashed raisin."

Grandpa

I've always left my keys in the tractor, or nearly always, but today they weren't there. This sort of thing happens to me. I misplace things, and it is so frustrating. I guess it is part of getting old. After checking the pockets of the clothes I wore yesterday, I came back out to get my work gloves off the tractor and there were my keys in the ignition. That is when I realized someone was playing tricks on Grandma and me. Thinking back, it wasn't difficult to figure out who.

Caleb

Katie and I continued our shenanigans throughout the day. My favorite was putting a little worm in Sophie's drink when she wasn't looking. She isn't normally afraid of worms, but having one floating in her lemonade made her scream and then get so red-faced and mad. Boy, can she get mad. I disappeared for a while until she cooled off.

Katie

Caleb and I have always had fun pulling jokes on people. After getting in trouble a few times, we have learned what is funny and what isn't. I hope. I feel a little bad about tricking Grandma when she works so hard for us, so we skipped putting plastic wrap over the toilet bowl. My favorite was popping the cap off the shampoo, covering the opening with plastic wrap, and then replacing the cap. You should have heard Molly yelling in the shower when she realized why the shampoo wouldn't come out.

Grandpa

I told the grandkids we were going to skip story time tonight. I said it had been a long hard day and Grandma and I were too tired. Then the phone rang. It was a setup. I acted sad while talking. Then I told Caleb and Katie they needed to pack their suitcases quickly because their mom and dad were almost here to pick them up. They wouldn't be coming inside because they needed to get back home before midnight. You should have seen their faces.

"What about Josh?" Katie asked.

"They didn't mention Josh," I said.

So Caleb and Katie quickly packed and sadly hugged everyone goodbye. They looked so forlorn sitting out on the steps all by themselves with their luggage. They sat. And sat. Caleb said they must be in big trouble. Katie reminded him Daddy had told them no shenanigans. In the meantime, I let the others in on the secret. Then we opened the door and hollered, "Gotcha!"

Caleb and Katie looked completely shocked and then started smiling as the cousins jumped and danced all over the place hollering "Gotcha, gotcha, gotcha!" There was lots of teasing and hugs, and everything was okay again.

~ *PART FOUR* ~

VACATION ENDS

LOSING A COUSIN AND THE LAST NIGHT

Caleb

Josh, Charlie, and I took the horses for a slow ride in the neighbor's field this morning. We didn't talk much and came back sooner than usual. We were tired. Thankfully, the girls wanted the horses, so we didn't need to unsaddle them. Usually, after a big day, we fall right to sleep, but last night, we three boys used our freedom to stay awake and quietly play "Risk," long after Elliott went to sleep.

Charlie wanted to get our midmorning snack and head for the creek. It was one of those warm, lazy mornings and I wasn't up to it. He insisted that we could find a cool spot and do nothing. Doing nothing didn't sound so bad, so that is what we did. Nothing. We did nothing. Or didn't do nothing. Ha! Anyway, Charlie is good at it. He can find a place, often in a tree, and just sit and look and listen for an hour or so. He says he does his best thinking up there. Elliott promised that if he could come along, he would do nothing, too. He left us alone and played in the water and along the banks.

I like listening to the sounds of nature, but this morning,

they lulled me to sleep while sitting on the damp ground and leaning against a big old cottonwood tree. Josh woke me and said we should be getting back for lunch. He had drifted off, too. So had Charlie. Good thing he hadn't been up in a tree or he might have fallen out on his head and wouldn't be thinking at all.

Elliott. Oh, no! Where was Elliott? Boy, did we panic and started calling as loudly as we could. Finally, we could hear his answer from quite a distance downstream. He had slowly meandered farther than he realized. Probably following a bug. It scared us, and when he came back, we really yelled at him for going so far off alone. He could have drowned or something. Our yelling at him really hurt his feelings. A brother is one thing, but cousins shouldn't do that. He started crying and said through big sobs that he was very careful and didn't mean to go so far. Besides, we weren't taking good care of him.

After giving *that* some thought, we talked it out so he would understand how worried and scared we were that something bad might have happened to him.

We all said we were sorry and decided we wouldn't tell about it when we got back to the house.

Well, Sophie took one look at her brothers' faces and asked what we boys had done at the creek.

"Nothin'" Charlie said, and quickly left the room.

"Nothin' and I wasn't good at it," Elliott said.

Katie

We don't have transportation to take the eleven of us to town at the same time, so Grandpa often takes one or two when he makes trips to get groceries. I rode with him this time, and we brought home pizza, marshmallows, graham crackers, and chocolate bars to celebrate our last night. We ate outside, and then made a campfire. It was fun roasting marshmallows and making s'mores while we talked. We even had our nightly story time before we went in.

CONCERNS

Grandma

It was our last night to have story time before bed, but the grandkids had some concerns.

"What will our parents say when they find out bobcats were here, and probably right where we had played?"

"And the rattlesnake?"

"And remember, Katie got bucked off the horse."

"Will they be mad that we could disappear for half a day without an adult with us?"

"Will we be allowed to come back again?"

Well, I wouldn't be telling the truth if I said I hadn't been a little worried about them. I am actually surprised we haven't taken someone in for stitches or for stepping on a nail. No broken bones from falling out of trees, either. More than anything, I'm proud of how they handled each situation. Yes, each one. So, I took the time to tell them so.

"Allison, you should be so proud of yourself for becoming more and more responsible for taking care of your diabetes. I'm amazed when I watch you fill the syringes with just the right amount of each type of insulin and give yourself shots in your stomach without even flinching. When you felt low, you took your blood sugar test, drank your juice, and avoided the fun until you were better. I hate you having diabetes, too, but I'm very proud of the way you put up with it and take care of yourself.

"Allison and Erin, you took responsibility for the horses and made sure they were saddled properly. You took care of Katie when she was bucked off and encouraged her to keep on riding. Then there was the time you girls saw the rattlesnake and remembered to notice landmarks so Grandpa could sneak up and shoot him. That is smart thinking under stressful circumstances.

"Josh and Caleb, being the older boys, you took responsibility for the chores and volunteered your help without us asking. You watched out for and encouraged the others when you were off on adventures. Grandpa and I believed everyone was in good hands.

"Katie, you are always a good balance for everyone. I noticed how you steal away to your favorite tree for your quiet time each day, and I can see how that helps you be such a sweet girl.

"Molly, you never sat around complaining if you weren't able to do something, but instead found ways to make your vacation enjoyable anyway. You are a happy person and often make the others laugh. That is a wonderful quality to have.

"Sophie, you are such a compassionate, caring person, and Grandpa and I are so happy you and Molly have become good buddies. We loved hearing the two of you chatting and giggling together.

"Charlie, I think you like the outdoors more than anyone, and I've heard you are the best tree climber. We are proud of you for hanging in there and holding your own with the older kids. Because you were persistent, you can even handle a hammer.

"Elliott, it is not just anyone who can be away from home for two whole weeks at your age, especially with disturbing things happening, such as an extra bad thunderstorm. Grandpa will always remember how the two of you became pals.

"How I appreciated all of you chipping in and being such good helpers with the loads of dirty clothes, cooking, cleaning, and gardening. You never waited until I asked, but always said, 'Grandma, is there something I can help you with?'

"Grandpa and I loved teaching all of you new skills and listening to your chatter and laughter. We had a wonderful time and feel so blessed you came. We are proud of each of you. As you grow older, you will make mistakes, but you can never do anything to lose our love. Always feel our love like a cuddly blanket wrapped around you, and come back often!"

TIME TO LEAVE

Grandma

Saturday morning came—again. And the parents arrived one at a time—again. They stayed until after lunch—again. Only this time, everyone was going to leave. However, it was a great reunion. I think the parents missed their children more than the other way around. Grandpa and I were overwhelmed with all the chatter. It seemed like everyone was talking at once, but we heard words like *horses, bugs, bobcat*, and *rattlesnake* now and then. And *freedom*.

Of course, Dolly got immediate attention.

The girls showed their crocheting and embroidered pillow cases. Elliott brought in his bug collection. And all of the cousins made their case to their parents about how helpful they had been while they were here. Then we all walked down to see the creek swing, the horses, the loft floor, and my deer stand.

Although organized, it was quite an event getting the cars loaded. They thanked us again and again for everything.

Enough hugs were given to keep our hug tanks full for days, maybe weeks. Grandpa gave each of the boys his very own hammer just as they left, and the kids all joined in on their rendition of "If I Had a Hammer" as they were pulling out.

"I bet that is going to drive their parents nuts," Grandpa said with a twinkle as everyone waved goodbye.

Soon, the last car pulled down the lane, and I heard my own mother's voice from so very long ago. I saw her as plain as if it were today as she hugged us and our four children. "The house will be so quiet when you are gone," she said.

Just as I remembered those times and those words, I am confident that her great-grandchildren, the nine first cousins, will always remember their two weeks at our farm and how special it is to be family.

~ PART FIVE ~

THANK YOU NOTES

NOTES OF THANKS FROM THE COUSINS

Grandma

Everyone likes to receive thank-you cards, don't you agree? At least good ones. You know, the cards that say more than just, "Thank you for the gift." Well, let me share the thank-you notes from our grandchildren.

FROM ALLISON, ERIN, AND MOLLY:

Allison

Hi, Grandpa and Grandma! This is a double thank-you note. Thanks for the card and money for my 13th birthday. I'm a teenager! Dad and Mom took me out to eat for my birthday and we had a grownup conversation. I guess it is scary for parents to have a teenager.

When we finished with the talk, I told them what you, Grandma, told us cousins about remembering. You know, you said that even when you get as old as you are, you still remember the things you did when you were young that you are ashamed of, things you wished you hadn't done, and to try to keep them to a minimum. I said I was going to try to keep mine to a minimum, and Mom and Dad hugged me. I love you both and thanks for every single thing. We first cousins had a great time, and that is worth remembering. Love, Allison

Erin

Grandpa and Grandma, I had the best time ever at the farm. It was like a two-week summer camp for only first cousins. We were so lucky. I learned a lot and had so much fun, too. I hope we didn't wear you out. Do you still have the horses? Do you ride them? My friends are jealous that I made my pretty scarf, and they want me to teach them how to crochet. Thanks for everything. Love, Erin

Molly

Dear Grandpa and Grandma, you are the best. Can we come again next summer? I like chickens and gathering eggs. I found out our city allows us to have five chickens. No roosters because they are too noisy. Mom and Dad are considering it. Mom says that I'm probably the only girl my age who is asking for my very own sewing machine for Christmas, and it isn't even Halloween yet. Love you, and thanks again for having us. Molly

FROM JOSH, CALEB, AND KATIE:

Josh

Thank you for letting all nine of us cousins come to the farm at the same time. We really had fun together, and I will always remember the many things we learned and did and how you trusted us. Well, I have to get cracking! Love, Josh

Caleb

Thank you for all the work you did while we were there. I loved building things and going exploring. Saddling and riding the horses was real special, too. Thank you also for free time. Grandma, did you sit up in the deer stand, yet? Love, Caleb

Katie

Thank you for teaching me on how to crochet, Grandma. I want to learn more the next time I see you. Thanks, also, for giving me the pillow case and teaching me how to embroider it. Allison, Erin, and I had so much fun on our horse rides. It was great being with girls instead of brothers. You both did so much work for us. I love you, Katie

Josh and Caleb

Oh, yeah, the hammers. Thanks for the hammers.

FROM CHARLIE, SOPHIE, AND ELLIOTT:

Charlie

Dear Grandpa and Grandma, I love your farm. Not every farm has a creek, a spring, and woods. I liked riding the horses, going tracking, climbing trees, swinging over the creek, and going out with the bigger kids on adventures.

I have to tell you about Elliott. He tells all his friends, and anyone who will listen, everything we did on the farm. It is like he was never scared or homesick, and it was the best adventure ever. He even carries a rattle from the snake in his pocket and tells people, "My grandpa shot the rattler to smithereens." I think it's so funny! Thanks again. Love you, Charlie

Sophie

Hi, Grandpa and Grandma, I miss you. And, I miss Molly. We Skype nearly every night. Dad calls it giggle time. Can we come again next summer? Thank you for all you taught me, for feeding me, and for washing my clothes. Mom says she doesn't know how you two did it all. See you at Christmas. Lots of hugs, Sophie

Elliott

Hi, Grandma and Grandpa, how is Dolly? Is she getting big? Does she sleep on the porch now? Will she remember me next time? Have you seen any more rattlesnakes or bobcats? I wish we had a swing over a creek and some horses. Thanks for taking good care of me. I had fun. I won't forget being there because I think about everything we did as I go to sleep at night. I love you, Grandpa and Grandma. Elliott

"A cousin is a little bit of childhood that can never be lost."

-Marion C. Garretty

ABOUT THE AUTHOR

Mary Moore Conley was raised on a farm in northwest Iowa, near the small town of Washta, She and husband Larry married young and moved to Omaha, Nebraska where he attended school. Their jobs kept them in Omaha where they raised their four children, and they now have the nine delightful grandchildren who are the characters in this book.

Mary and husband bought a little hobby farm when they were in their mid-sixties and became quite consumed with cleaning it up and rebuilding. It is now their passion to grow most of their produce organically.

Mary is happiest when she is writing, and writing children's books has always been a dream of hers. This book has brought her much joy and it is her hope that you will like it, too.

She can be reached at 9firstcousins@cox.net

Made in the USA
Columbia, SC
18 February 2018